To Stanford Nursery School

Henry Holt and Company, LLC
PUBLISHERS SINCE 1866
175 Fifth Avenue
New York, New York 10010
www.HenryHoltKids.com

Henry Holt® is a registered trademark of Henry Holt and Company, LLC.
Copyright © 2009 by Peter McCarty
All rights reserved.
Distributed in Canada by H. B. Fenn and Company Ltd.

Library of Congress Cataloging-in-Publication Data
McCarty, Peter.
Jeremy draws a monster / Peter McCarty.—1st ed.
p.   cm.
Summary: A young boy who spends most of his time alone in his bedroom makes new friends
after the monster in his drawing becomes a monstrous nuisance.
ISBN-13: 978-0-8050-6934-1 / ISBN-10: 0-8050-6934-8
[1. Monsters—Fiction. 2. Drawing—Fiction. 3. Loneliness—Fiction] I. Title.
PZ7.M47841327Je 2009   [E]—dc22   2008036813

First Edition—2009 / Designed by Patrick Collins
The artist used pen and ink and watercolors on watercolor paper to create the illustrations for this book.
Printed in February 2009 in the United States of America by Worzalla,
Stevens Point, Wisconsin, on acid-free paper. ∞

1   3   5   7   9   10   8   6   4   2

For Matthew

Jeremy
Draws a
Monster

Peter McCarty

Henry Holt and Company
NEW YORK

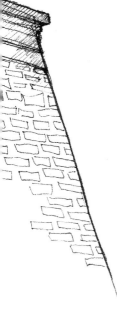

J eremy lived on the top floor
of a three-story apartment building.

He had his very own room.
He never left. He never went outside.

One day, Jeremy took out his fancy pen
and started to draw. He began at the top...

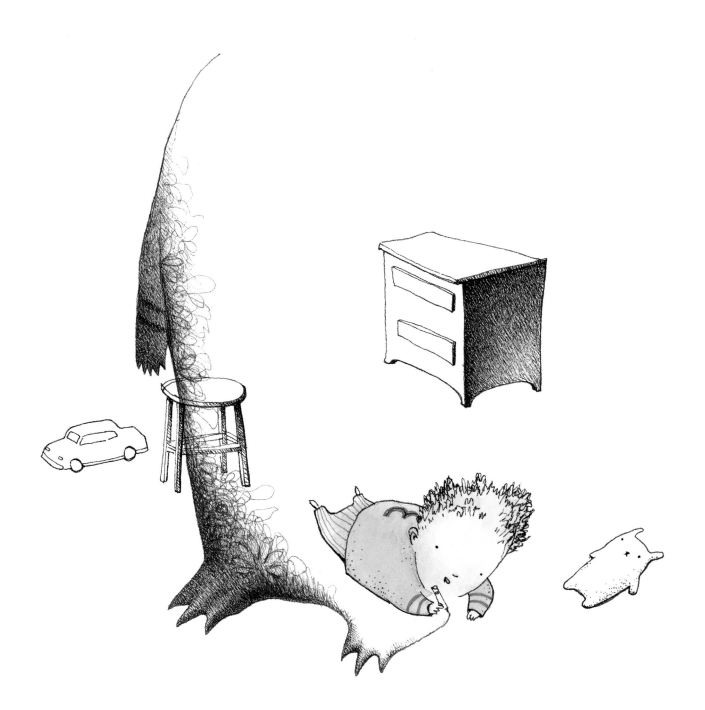

and continued over to the other side.

Jeremy drew

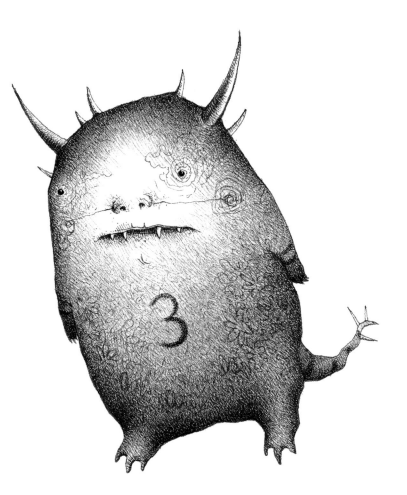

a monster.

"Arrgh," said the monster.
"Draw me a sandwich. I'm hungry!"

The monster did not say thank you.

"Draw me a toaster," growled
the monster. "I like toast.
Draw me a record player.
It's too quiet around here!
Draw me a checkerboard.
I want to play checkers.
Draw me a comfortable chair."

"Draw me a television. I want to watch the game. And draw me a hot dog too.

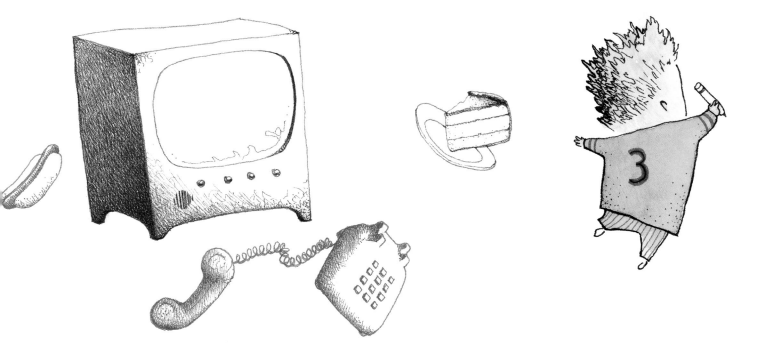

Draw me a telephone. Somebody might call.
Draw me a piece of cake. I want dessert!"

Then the monster said, "Are you going to sit there all day? Draw me a hat. I'm going out!"

Jeremy was relieved that the
monster was gone.

Later that night, Jeremy heard
BANG! BANG! BANG! at the door.

The monster had returned.

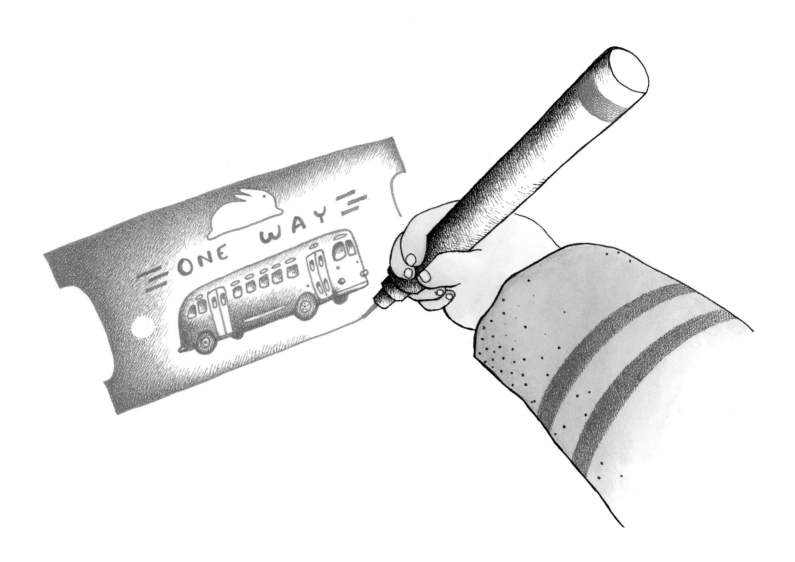

The next morning, Jeremy drew a bus
ticket and a suitcase.

Jeremy led the monster out the door,
down the stairs to the street,

and onto the next bus
out of town.

"Do you want to play ball?"
asked the neighbors.

"Okay," Jeremy said.

And they did.